# To the Sea

by Cale Atkinson

Disney • HYPERION

Los Angeles   New York

Dedicated to anyone who feels invisible and
any whale that needs to get back to the sea.

First Edition, May 2015
10 9 8 7 6 5 4 3 2 1
H106-9333-5-15032

Printed in Malaysia

Library of Congress Cataloging-in-Publication Data

Atkinson, Cale.
To the sea / Cale Atkinson.—First edition.
pages cm
Summary: Tim, a boy, and Sam, a blue whale lost in the city, both feel unnoticed until they meet,
and they become best friends as Tim tries to help Sam get back home.
ISBN 978-1-4847-0813-2—ISBN 1-4847-0813-X
[1. Best friends—Fiction. 2. Friendship—Fiction.
3. Blue whale—Fiction. 4. Whales—Fiction.] I. Title.
PZ7.A86372To 2015
[E]—dc23          2014015783

Reinforced binding
Visit www.DisneyBooks.com

This is Tim.

One day  after school...

Tim met Sam.

Sam lived in the sea
but took a wrong turn
and got stuck here.

He didn't know his
← lefts from his rights. →

The other kids were too busy to notice the big blue whale.

Sometimes
Tim felt no one
noticed him either.

"I see you," said Tim.
"I see you too,"
said Sam.

They both felt
better knowing
they weren't
invisible.

Tim went back into the school
to get a glass of water for Sam,
since whales love their water.

He didn't care
anymore if no one
noticed him,

because now
Sam did.

Tim asked Sam,
"Do you want to be my friend?"

And Sam did.

Sam told his friend that
he didn't know how to get
back home to the sea.

Tim promised to
help Sam get
to the sea.

"I pinkie-swear."

Tim had to go home but said he would be back tomorrow.

He left Sam two glasses of water, some company, and kept one light on.

At home, Tim
couldn't stop
thinking about
Sam.

It's not
every day
you meet
a friend.

He spent all
night planning
how to get
Sam to the
sea.

The next day
Sam was excited to see his friend again.
"You came back!"

"Of course,"
said Tim.

"Friends don't
let friends down."

Tim showed Sam his plans.

sam

"We could drive...."

"Or maybe even fly...."

"Well, I don't have a car," said Sam,
"and I'm a little afraid of heights...."

Just when it looked like none of his ideas would work...

Tim came across the very last one.

Sam held on extra tight.

Tim began to pedal,

but Sam didn't move.

Tim didn't
give up.

Sam was his only friend.
His best friend.


He should not,
he could not,
he would not let his
friend down.

Tim pedaled harder, and they started to move.

Tim pedaled harder, and soon they were passing buses and cars!

Tim pedaled harder, and soon they were going too fast to see...

and too fast to stop!

Tim sank deep into the sea

and could not

see Sam

anywhere.

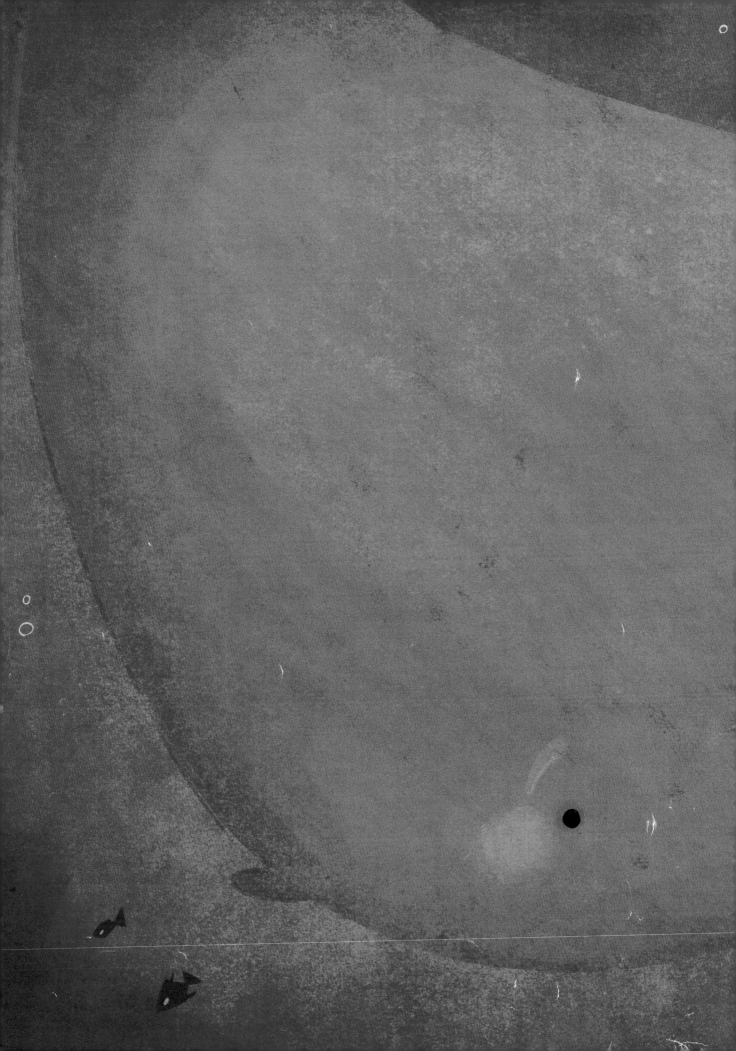

"I see you,"
said Sam.

"You came back!"

"Of course I did!
Friends don't let friends down."

It's not every day you meet
a new friend,

and it's not every day
they meet you.

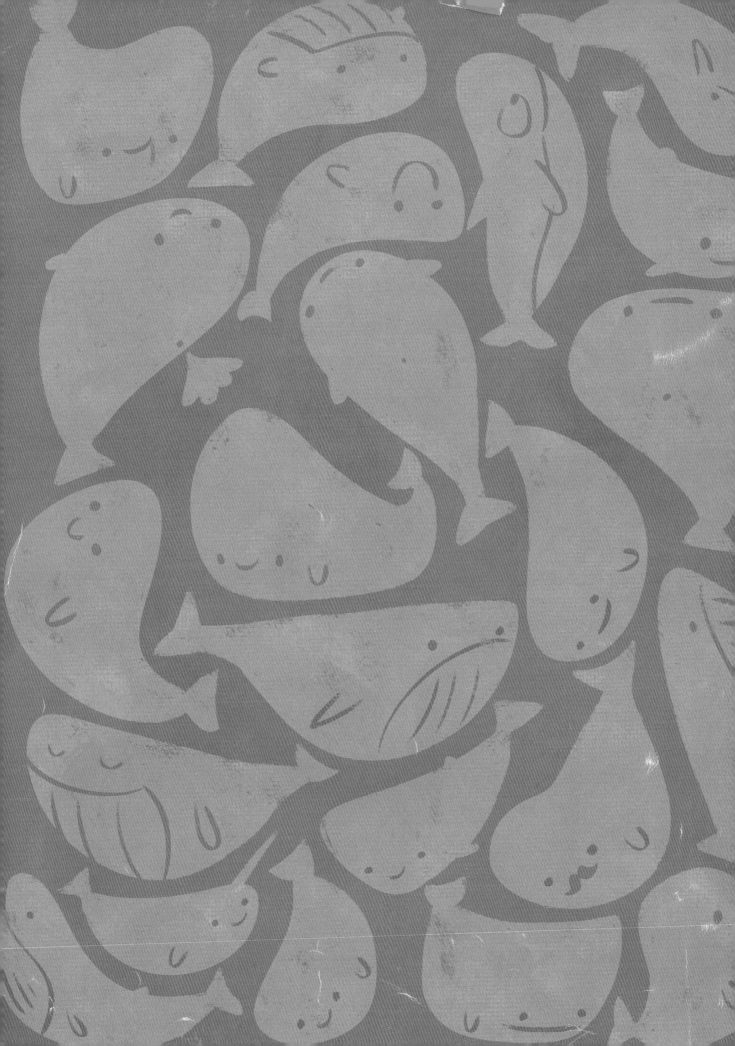